THE
STEADFAST
TIN SOLDIER

HANS CHRISTIAN ANDERSEN

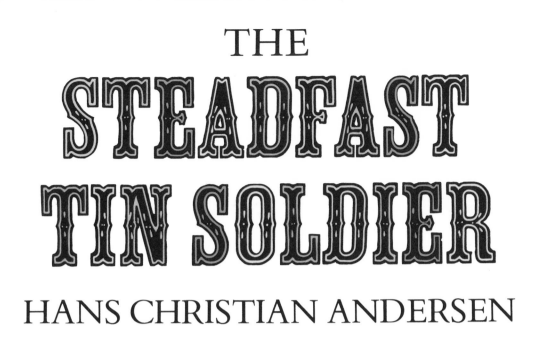

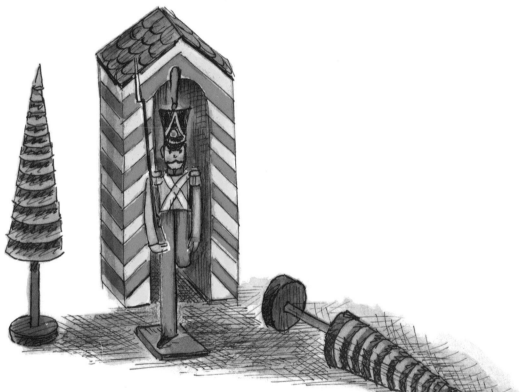

illustrated by Paul Galdone

Houghton Mifflin/Clarion Books/New York

To Jim, Marjorie,
Isabel, Olga and Vikki

Printed in the United States of America

Library of Congress Cataloging in Publication Data

Andersen, Hans Christian, 1805-1875.
The steadfast tin soldier.
Translation of Den standhaftige tinsoldat.
Summary: After being accidentally launched on a dangerous and terrible voyage, a one-legged soldier finds his way back to his true love—a paper dancing girl.
[1. Fairy tales] I. Galdone, Paul. II. Title.
PZ8.A542St   1979   [E]   79-4325   ISBN 0-395-28964-5

There once were five and twenty tin soldiers. They were all brothers for they had all been made from the same old tin spoon. They shouldered their muskets and looked straight ahead, splendid in their red and blue uniforms.

The first thing they heard in the world, when the lid was taken off their box, was a little boy clapping his hands and crying, "Tin soldiers!"

It was the little boy's birthday and the tin soldiers had just been given to him. He set them up on the table.

All the soldiers were alike except one. He had only one leg. He was the last of the soldiers to be cast and there had not been quite enough tin left to finish him.

But he stood just as steadily on his one leg as the others did on their two. It was he who became famous.

On the table where the soldiers were set up were many other toys, but what first caught the eye was a delightful castle made of cardboard. Through the windows you could look right into the rooms. In front of the castle were some little trees surrounding a mirror lake. The surface reflected the small wax swans swimming about on it.

This was all very pretty, but the prettiest thing of all was the little ballerina who was standing at the open door of the castle. She, too, was cut out of cardboard. But she had a skirt of the finest gauze and over her shoulders, like a scarf, she wore a narrow blue ribbon. And in the middle of the ribbon was a tinsel rose.

The little ballerina stretched out both her arms, and she lifted one leg so high that the tin soldier could not see it at all. He supposed that she, like himself, had only one leg.

"That would be the wife for me," thought he, "but she is much too grand and lives in a castle. I have only a box and that belongs to the whole twenty five of us. It is no place for someone as fine as she. But I would like to make her acquaintance all the same!"

The soldier was partly hidden by a snuff-box which stood on the table. From there he could easily watch the ballerina who kept standing on one leg without ever losing her balance.

When evening came, the little boy put all the other tin soldiers in their box, and the people of the house went to bed. Now was the time for the toys to play. They visited one another and gave balls. The tin soldiers rattled in their box, for they wanted to join in the fun, but they could not get the lid off.

The nutcrackers turned somersaults and the pencil scribbled on the slate. There was such a noise that the canary bird woke up and joined in the chatter.

The only two who did not move from their places were the tin soldier and the little ballerina. She stood stiff as ever on tiptoe, with her arms spread out. The tin soldier stood just as steadily on his one leg and he did not take his eyes off her for a moment.

The clock struck twelve. Pop! Up went the lid of the snuff-box, but there was no snuff in it. Instead, out bounced a goblin disguised as a jack-in-the-box.

"Tin soldier!" said the goblin. "Stop staring at the ballerina! Keep your eyes to yourself!"

But the tin soldier pretended not to hear.

"Just you wait till tomorrow," said the goblin.

When the little boy got up in the morning, he put the tin soldier on the window sill. Whether it was the goblin or a puff of wind that did it, I do not know, but all at once the window burst open and the soldier fell head over heels from the third story! He fell down at a terrific speed and landed cap first,with his leg in the air and his bayonet stuck between the paving stones.

The little boy and a servant ran down at once to look for him. They nearly stepped on him, but they failed to see him. If the soldier had cried out, "Here I am!" they would have found him. But he did not think it proper to cry out loudly when he was in uniform.

Then it began to rain. The drops fell heavier and heavier until it became a downpour.

When it was over, two boys came along.

"Just look," said one. "Here's a tin soldier. Let's send him for a sail."

So they made a boat out of a newspaper and put the soldier in the middle of it. Off he went, sailing down the gutter. The two boys ran alongside, clapping their hands. Good heavens! What waves there were in the gutter, and what a fast current!

The paper boat danced up and down and now and then whirled round and round, until the tin soldier was quite dizzy. But he was steadfast and didn't move a muscle. He just looked straight in front of him and shouldered his musket.

All at once the boat drifted into a long drainpipe. It was just as dark as the box the tin soldier has shared with his brothers.

"Where am I going now?" he thought. "It must all be that goblin's fault."

Suddenly a great water rat who lived in the drainpipe
swam up.

"Where's your pass?" asked the rat. "Let me have it."

The tin soldier did not speak but clung still tighter to his musket. The boat rushed on past the floating bits of straw and wood. The rat, close behind, gnashed his teeth and shouted, "Stop him! Stop him! He hasn't shown his pass! He hasn't paid the toll!"

But the current grew stronger and stronger. The tin soldier began to see daylight before him at the end of the tunnel. But he could also hear a roaring sound that was enough to strike terror in the boldest heart. For just where the tunnel ended the stream poured out into a wide canal. He was already so near it that he could not possibly stop.

The paper boat was swept out into the canal, and the poor tin soldier held himself as stiff as he could. He never even moved an eyelid. The boat whirled around three or four times, filled with water to the very brim, and began to sink. The tin soldier stood up to his neck in water, and the boat sank deeper and deeper.

The paper became limper and limper and at last the water closed over the soldier's head. He thought of the pretty little ballerina whom he would never see again. And in his ears rang this refrain from an old song:

> *Oh warrior bold, goodbye!*
> *Thy end, alas, is nigh.*

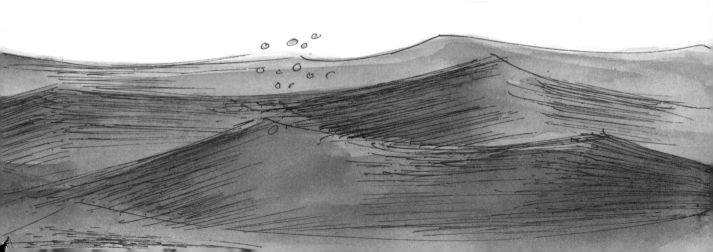

Then the paper gave way, and the soldier fell through
the bottom. But at that moment he was snapped up by a
great fish.

Oh, how dark it was inside the fish! It was even darker than in the drainpipe and there was so little room. But the tin soldier was as steadfast as ever and lay full length, shouldering his musket.

Then the fish turned and twisted about and made the strangest movements. At last it became quite still and a long time passed. Then suddenly there was a flash like lightning. The soldier was once more in broad daylight and someone cried, "Tin soldier!"

The fish had been caught, taken to the market, sold, and brought to the kitchen, where the cook had just cut it open with a big knife. She picked up the soldier by the waist and marched him into the sitting room. Everyone was eager to see the little man who had been traveling about inside a fish. But the tin soldier was not at all proud.

They stood him up on a table and, wonder of wonders, he found himself in the very same room where he had been before. He saw the same little boy with his brothers and sisters, and the same toys standing on the table. And there was the same pretty castle with the graceful little ballerina in the doorway.

She still stood on one leg and held the other high in the air. She was also steadfast. The soldier was so moved that he was ready to shed tears, but that would not have been proper. He looked at her and she at him, but neither spoke a word.

Then one of the little children grabbed the tin soldier, flung him into the stove, and slammed the door. He had no reason for doing this. It must have been the fault of the goblin in the snuff-box.

The tin soldier stood in a blaze of red light and felt a great heat, but whether it was from the fire or from love he did not know. He could feel himself melting, but he still stood firm, shouldering his musket.

Suddenly the door of the stove was flung open, and the little boy reached in, trying to rescue the tin soldier. But the fire was too hot.

At that moment a draft caught hold of the little ballerina. It swept her straight into the stove next to the tin soldier. She blazed up into a flame, and was gone.

The soldier melted. When the maid came to take out the ashes the next day, she found him in the shape of a little tin heart. Beside the heart was the ballerina's tinsel rose, burned black as a cinder.

R00158 72802

12 PEACHTREE

J
P
A

Andersen, H. C. (Hans Christian),
1805-1875.
The steadfast tin soldier / Hans
Christian Andersen ; illustrated by
Paul Galdone. -- New York : Houghton
Mifflin/Clarion Books, c1979.
[32] p. : col. ill. ; 26 cm.
Translation of Den standhaftige
tinsoldat.

07/08/86

0531437
Card 1 of 2